For Isobel and Tom ~ DB

For all the little bears in my world ~ CP

This edition published by Scholastic Inc., 557 Broadway; New York, NY 10012,
by arrangement with Little Tiger Press.
SCHOLASTIC and associated logos are trademarks and/or
registered trademarks of Scholastic Inc.
Scholastic Canada Ltd.; Markham, Ontario

First published in the United States by Good Books, Intercourse, PA 17534, 2007

Library of Congress Cataloging-in-Publication Data is available for this title.

Original edition published in English by Little Tiger Press,
an imprint of Magi Publications, London, England, 2007

Text copyright © David Bedford 2007
Illustrations copyright © Caroline Pedler 2007

ISBN-10: 1-84506-836-X; ISBN-13: 978-1-84506-836-3

Printed in China

2 4 6 8 10 9 7 5 3 1

Bedtime
for Little Bears!

David Bedford   Caroline Pedler

Little Bear and his mother
had spent a long, sunny
day exploring in the snow.

"It's getting late," said Mother Bear. "It will soon be bedtime. Let's go home, Little Bear."

Little Bear flumped down in the snow and wiggled his tail. "I'm not sleepy," he said, "and I don't want to go to bed yet."

Mother Bear smiled. "Shall we take one last walk," she said, "and see who else is going to bed?"

Little Bear looked around. "Who else *is* going to bed?" he wondered.

Mother Bear stretched up tall to find out.

"Look there," she said.

"It's Little Owl!" said Little Bear.

"Little Owl likes to stretch her wings before bedtime, and feel the whisper of the soft night breeze in her feathers," said Mother Bear.

Little Bear scrambled onto his
mother's shoulders.

"I like flying too!" he said.

As Mother Bear climbed to the
top of a hill, Little Bear felt the
wind whispering and tickling
through his fur.

Then he saw someone else . . . .

"Who's that?" said Little Bear, giggling. "And what's he doing?"

"Baby Hare is having a bath in the snow," said Mother Bear, "so that he's clean and drowsy, and ready for sleep."

"I like snow baths too," said Little Bear. He dived into the snow and scattered it around, plopping a big, soft snowball on Mother Bear's nose.

Little Bear and his
mother laughed as they
flopped down together
in a heap.

"Are you sleepy now, Little
Bear?" his mother asked as they
lay together in the snow,
watching the first bright stars
twinkling in the sky.

Little Bear blinked his tired eyes as he tried not to yawn. "I want to see who else is going to bed," he said.

"We'll have to be quiet now," said Mother Bear. "Some little ones will already be asleep."

"Look over there," whispered Mother Bear. "Little Fox likes being cuddled and snuggled to sleep by his mother."

Little Bear pressed close against Mother Bear's warm fur. "I like cuddles too," he said.

"We'll be home soon," said his mother softly.

But Little Bear had just seen somebody else . . . .

"I can see whales!" he said, turning to look out
across the starlit sea.

"Little Whale likes his mother to sing him softly
to sleep," said Mother Bear.

Little Bear sat with his mother and watched the
whales swimming by until they were gone, leaving
only the soothing hum of their far-away song.
Then he yawned. "Are we nearly home yet?" he
said drowsily.

Little Bear climbed onto his mother's back, and as he was carried home he watched the colors that flickered and brushed across the sky, while his mother sang him a lullaby.

"I like songs too," he told his mother.

"And now," said Mother Bear very softly, "it's time for little bears to go to sleep."

Little Bear nestled into his mother's soft fur, and when she gave him a gentle kiss goodnight . . .

. . . Little Bear was
already fast asleep.